STEVEN UNIVERSE
A CARTOON NETWORK ORIGINAL

Fusion for Beginners and Experts

by STEVEN and GARNET

CARTOON NETWORK BOOKS
Penguin Young Readers Group
An Imprint of Penguin Random House LLC

STEVEN UNIVERSE, CARTOON NETWORK, the logos and all related characters and elements are
trademarks of and © Cartoon Network. (s17). All rights reserved. Published in 2017 by Cartoon Network
Books, an imprint of Penguin Random House LLC, 345 Hudson Street, New York, New York 10014.
Manufactured in China.

ISBN 9781524784690   10 9 8 7 6 5 4 3 2 1

Fusion for Beginners and Experts

by Rebecca Sugar and Angie Wang

illustrated by Angie Wang

An Imprint of Penguin Random House

There are a bunch of great reasons to fuse:

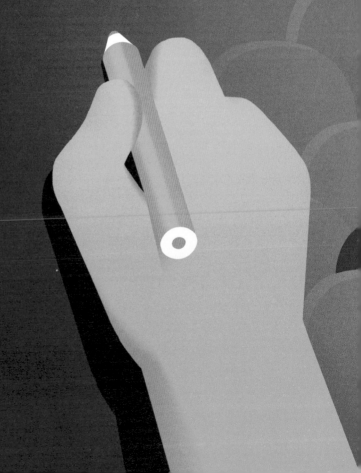

To gain
a different...

...perspective!

Because you
have great...

...chemistry!

Because together you're more...

...powerful!

You might want to fuse

because you're so...

...alike!

Or you might want to fuse

because
you're so...

...different!

You don't have to agree on

everything in
order to fuse,

but you *must* agree...

...that you
want to fuse!

And if you don't want to fuse...

...that's cool, too.

Fusion is not always easy,

or right,

or good,

or forever.

And yet—

What will you learn...

...if you fuse?

What a surprise

the brilliant shapes

you
create

Together,

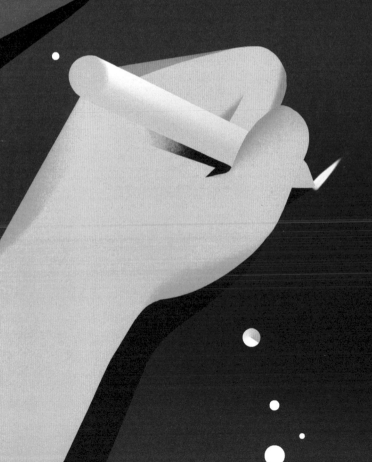

but
still you—

You—

yet
someone

entirely
new.

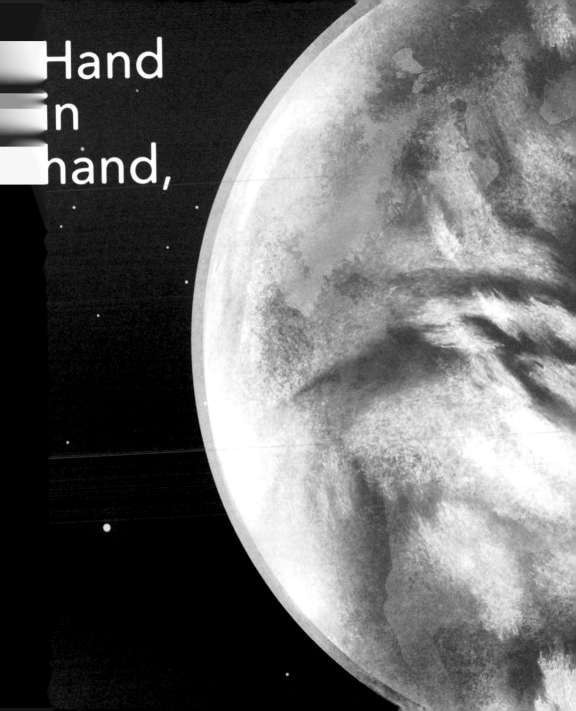

Hand
in
hand,

gem
to
gem,

you make
your home on
this planet—

in each other.